Adapted by Rebecca Potters

ISBN 978-1-338-70143-2

10 9 8 7 6 5 4 3 2 1   21 22 23 24 25

Printed in the U.S.A.   40
First printing 2021
Book design by Jessica Meltzer

SCHOLASTIC INC.

It's Easter at Rainbow Kindi. Ms. R Bow has a surprise for the Kindi Kids.

"Today we will be decorating Easter eggs," Ms. R Bow explains. "Then we'll share our decorations."

The Kindi Kids clap. They are excited!

Jessicake has an idea for her egg.

"My favorite thing is to play, so I think I'll draw some games on my egg," she says.

"Did someone say **PLAY**?" Donatina asks.

The Kindi Kids do the Bobble Dance. They even add a new hop to the dance moves, just like the Easter Bunny would!

Jessicake's favorite games are hopscotch, puzzles, and the Bobble Dance. She draws each of them on her egg.

Peppa-Mint's favorite thing in the world is peppermint ice cream.

She builds a device that makes her egg smell yummy—just like peppermint!

Donatina loves her bow. It's pink, just like her hair.

"Ooh, I have an idea!" Donatina shouts. "I'll make this Easter celebration a true fashion show."

She pulls out some ribbon and begins to craft.

9

Marsha Mello loves fluffy, sweet things, like clouds and cream puffs.

She decides to paint her egg! She paints it with everything fluffy she can think of.

Summer Peaches loves her popsicle. She uses it to sponge paint her egg with her favorite color—peach!

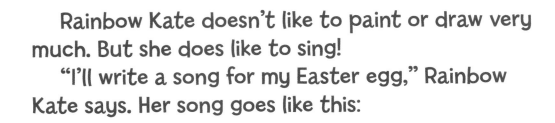

Rainbow Kate doesn't like to paint or draw very much. But she does like to sing!

"I'll write a song for my Easter egg," Rainbow Kate says. Her song goes like this:

13

When everyone is done, it's time to share their eggs.

The Kindi Kids line up.

"Oh, your egg is the loveliest, Donatina!" Jessicake shouts. "No, *yours* is the best," cuts in Rainbow Kate.

"Easter isn't about what's the best or the loveliest," Marsha Mello says. "Easter is about celebrating with your best friends."

"I have an idea!" says Summer Peaches. "Let's combine all our eggs together into a **MEGA EASTER EGG**? That way we'll have *one* egg for Rainbow Kindi, and inside of it, a bunch of different eggs for each one of us!"

Beary Chill decides to help the Kindi Kids with their **MEGA EASTER EGG**. He helps them glue it all together with cotton candy!

Then Bunny Cart helps the Kindi Kids by measuring her wheels. She makes an exact model of them—big enough for the **MEGA EASTER EGG!**

"Now it's a Mega Easter Egg on wheels!" Bunny Cart says.

The Kindi Kids giggle. Then they finish their **MEGA EASTER EGG**! Each Kindi Kid uses her own talent to make it as pretty as it can be.

"It's perfect," Jessicake says, looking at the MEGA EASTER EGG. "This is the best Easter egg ever."

"And it's all because we had each other!" shouts Rainbow Kate.

The Kindi Kids smile.

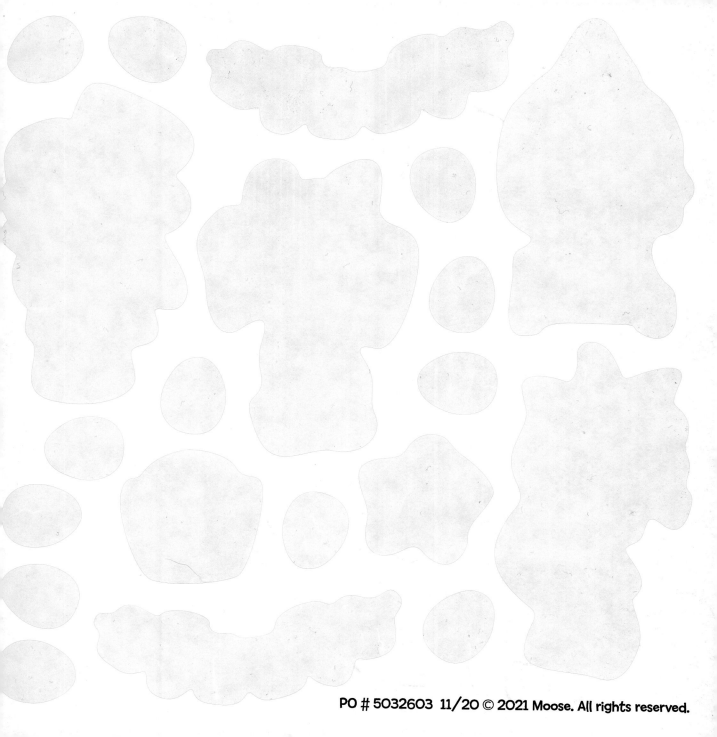